By Chris Raschka

A Richard Jackson Book

Atheneum Books for Young Readers

New York London Toronto Sydney

Little
Black
Crow

ATHENEUM BOOKS FOR YOUNG READERS
An imprint of Simon & Schuster Children's Publishing Division
1230 Avenue of the Americas, New York, New York 10020

For information about special discounts for bulk purchases,
please contact Simon & Schuster Special Sales at 1-866-506-1949 or
business@simonandschuster.com.
The Simon & Schuster Speakers Bureau can bring authors to your live event.
For more information or to book an event, contact the Simon & Schuster Speakers
Bureau at 1-866-248-3049 or visit our website at www.simonspeakers.com.
Book design by Ann Bobco
The text for this book is set in Ad Lib BT.
The illustrations for this book are rendered in watercolor and ink.
Manufactured in China
0910 SCP
4 6 8 10 9 7 5 3
Library of Congress Cataloging-in-Publication Data
Raschka, Christopher.
Little black crow / Chris Raschka. —1st ed.
p. cm.
"A Richard Jackson Book."
Summary: A boy thinks about the life of a little black crow that he sees,
wondering where it goes in the snow, where it sleeps,
and whether or not it worries like he does.
ISBN 978-0-689-84601-4 (hardcover)
[1. Stories in rhyme. 2. Crows—Fiction.] I. Title.
PZ8.3.R1768Li 2010
[E]—dc22
2009032110

for Lydie

Little black crow,
where do you go?

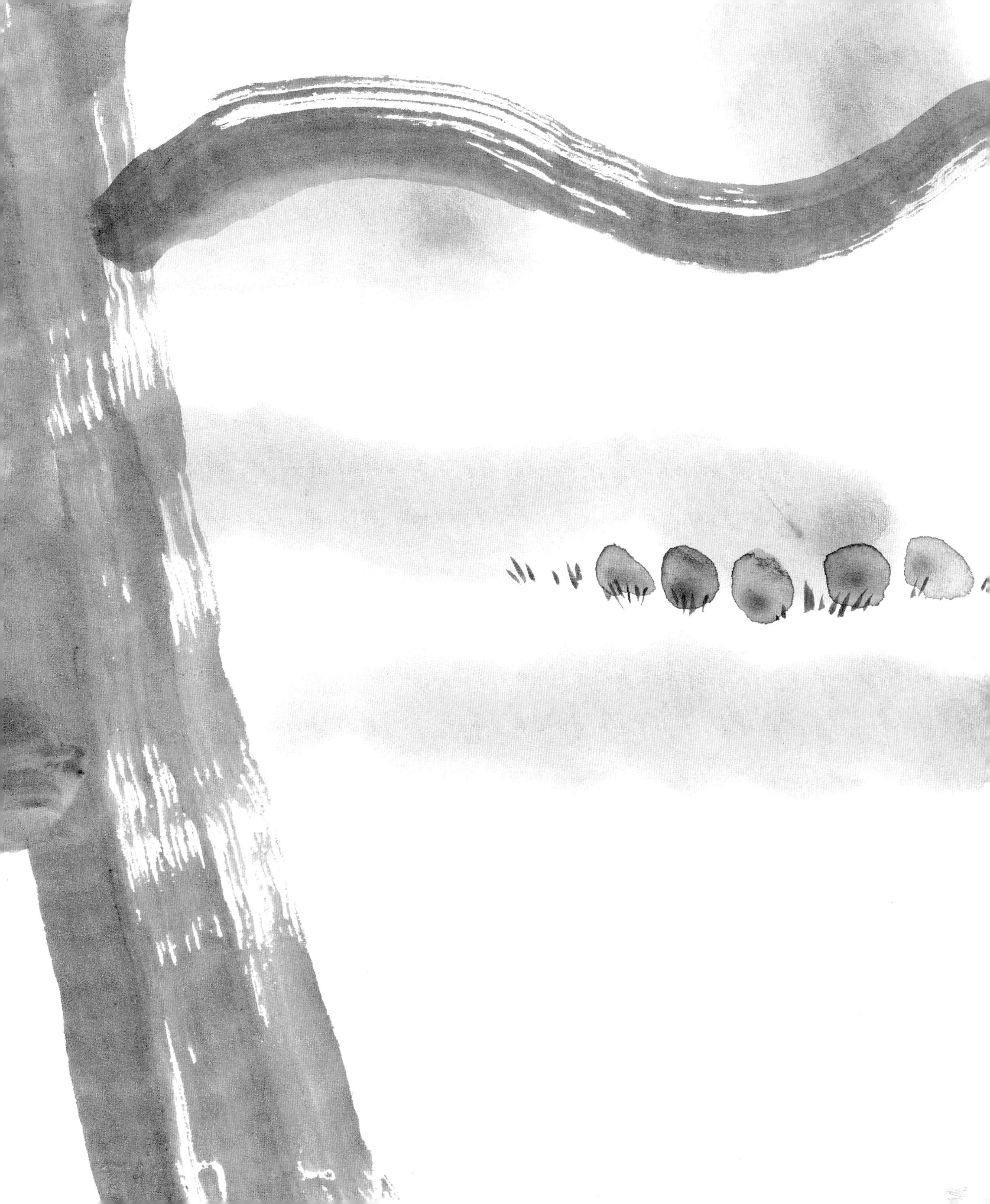

**Where do you go
in the cold white snow?**

Where do you go?

Little black crow,
where do you fly
in the stormy sky?

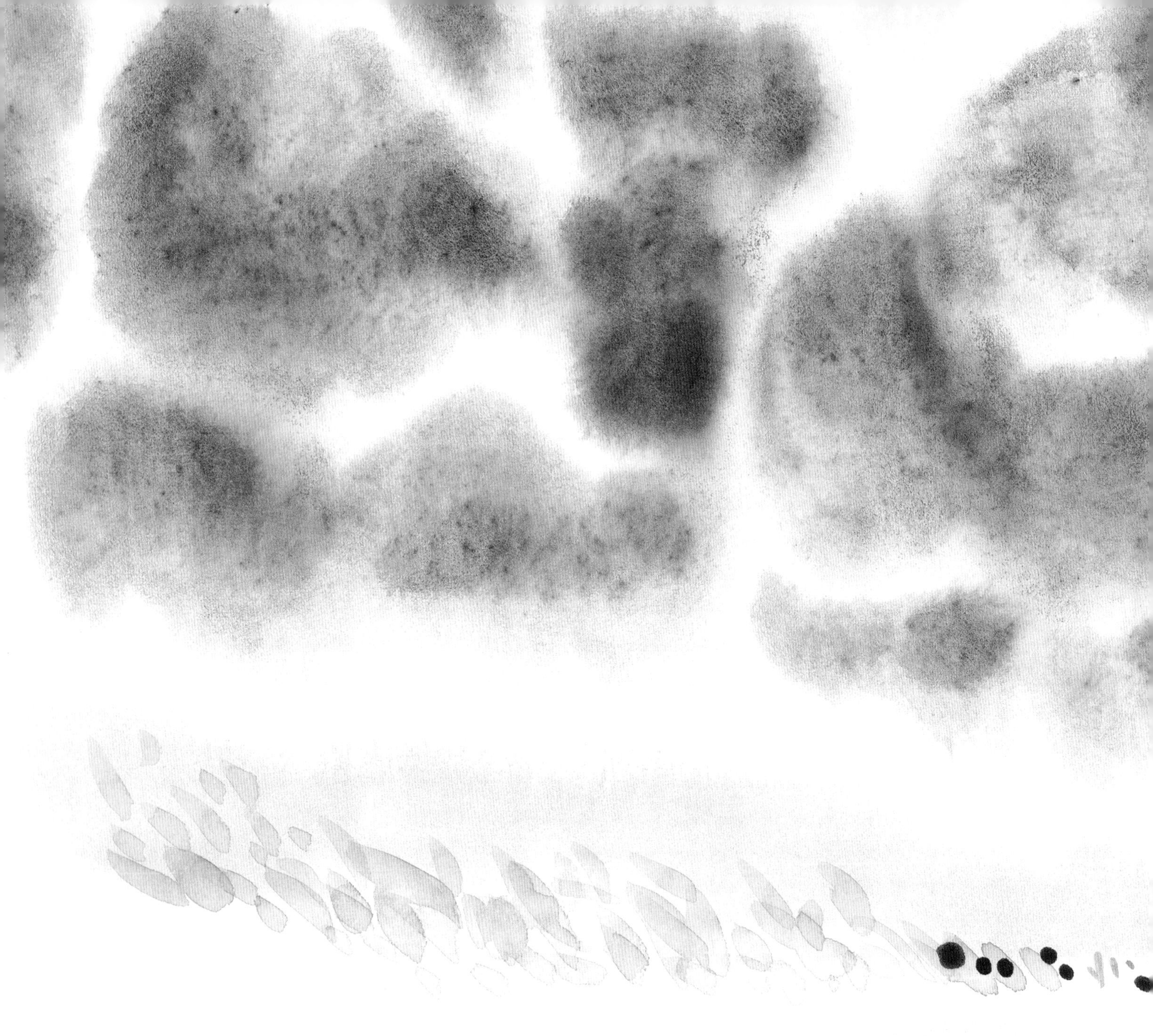

Whom do you meet
in the long wet street?
Whom do you meet?

Little black crow,
do you ever complain
in the wind
and the rain?
Do you ever complain?

Is it enough
to have feathers
in all kinds of
weathers?

Is it enough
to have feathers?

Little black crow
in that tall tree,
are you a boy like me?

With a sister and a brother and a father and a mother?

Are you a boy like me?

**Little black crow,
how do you sleep
in the forest so deep?
How do you sleep?**

Do you ever worry
when you hop
and you hurry?
Are you ever afraid
of mistakes you've made?

Are you never afraid?

**Little black crow,
whom do you love
in the clouds above?**

Whom do you love?

Is it that little gray dove?
Is that whom you love?

Little black crow,

do you ever wonder
about lightning
or thunder?

About morsels
you eat?
About creatures
you meet?

Little black crow
in the white snow
in the blue sky
in the brown below,

do you ever wonder
about stars you see?
Might you ever wonder
about someone . . .

. . . like me?